CHICAGO PUBLIC LIBRARY
SULZER REGIONAL
4455 N. LINCOLN
CHICAGO, IL 60625

JUV
FIC

SULZER

W9-BTE-396

R0400536966

Stuart goes to school

DATE DUE

DISCARD

NOV 2004

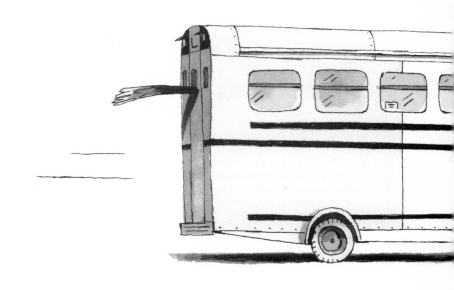

STUART
GOES TO
SCHOOL

BY SARA PENNYPACKER

ILLUSTRATED BY MARTIN MATJE

ORCHARD BOOKS

AN IMPRINT OF SCHOLASTIC INC.

NEW YORK

Text copyright © 2003 by Sara Pennypacker
Illustrations copyright © 2003 by Martin Matje

All rights reserved. Published by Orchard Books, an imprint of Scholastic Inc. ORCHARD BOOKS and design are registered trademarks of Watts Publishing Group, Ltd., used under license. SCHOLASTIC and associated logos are trademarks and/or registered trademarks of Scholastic Inc.

No part of this publication may be reproduced, or stored in a retrieval system, or transmitted in any form or by any means, electronic, mechanical, photocopying, recording, or otherwise, without written permission of the publisher. For information regarding permission, write to Orchard Books, Scholastic Inc., Attention: Permissions Department, 557 Broadway, New York, NY 10012.

LIBRARY OF CONGRESS CATALOGING-IN-PUBLICATION DATA

Pennypacker, Sara
Stuart Goes to School / by Sara Pennypacker; illustrated by Martin Matje. — 1 st ed.   p.   cm.
Summary: Worried about his first day at a new school, eight-year-old Stuart wears his magic cape and hopes that it will help him.

ISBN 0-439-30182-3
[1. First day of school —Fiction. 2. Worry —Fiction. 3. Clothing and dress —Fiction. 4. Magic —Fiction.]
I. Matje, Martin, ill. II. Title. PZ7.P3856 Sm 2002
[Fic] —dc21   2001049781   CIP AC

10 9 8 7 6 5 4 3 2 1   03 04 05 06 07

Printed in the United States of America   23

First edition, July 2003

The text type was set in 12-pt. Sabon.
Title type was handlettered by Martin Matje.
Display type was set in Bad Cabbage ICG.
Book design by Marijka Kostiw

R0400536966

For my guys, Hilly and Caleb.
—S. P.

To my mother, who gave me my cape.
—M. M.

CHICAGO PUBLIC LIBRARY
SULZER REGIONAL
4455 N. LINCOLN
CHICAGO, IL 60625

DAY ONE

As soon as he woke up, Stuart knew it was going to be a bad day. You can smell a bad day coming. It smells a lot like sour milk.

The first bad thing about the day was hanging on his bedpost. A pair of green plaid pants, so bright they hurt his eyes. A shirt with little cowboys on it.

Stuart was excellent at worrying. In fact, worrying was his best thing. But he had forgotten to worry about

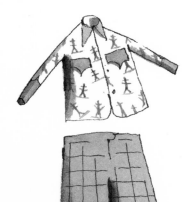

First day of School Suit

this. Every year, his mother made him dress up for the first day of school. In clothes nobody else would wear.

Stuart and his family had just moved to Punbury. He would be new at school, so he already had plenty to worry about. What if he forgot everything he learned in second grade? What if he couldn't find the bathroom? What if he *could* find the bathroom, but he got stuck inside and the teacher had to get him out with *firemen?* What if nobody wanted to be his friend?

And now this: green plaid hurt-your-eyes pants and a cowboy shirt. Where did his mother even *find* clothes like these?

"Stuart," he heard his mother call. "I left you a nice new outfit. It was your father's when he was in third grade! Now isn't *that* something?"

Stuart buried himself under his quilt. It would be impossible to make friends now. The other kids were going to fall down left and right laughing at him. Even cowboys would fall down left and right laughing at him.

He poked his head back out.

Wait a minute. He had a cape now. He had made it last week out of a hundred old ties. Just as he'd hoped, magical things had been happening since he had started wearing it. Adventures. A different one each day.

So far, the magical thing of the day had been a surprise. But *maybe*. . . .

Stuart pointed his brain at the ugly outfit. He squeezed his eyes shut and concentrated powerful brain waves on making it *disappear*. He concentrated hard until he smelled brain-smoke coming from behind his eyeballs. He opened his eyes.

The outfit was still there. It looked more horrible than before.

Stuart sighed deeply and got out of bed. He put on the awful clothes and wrapped his cape around himself. One good thing about a cape: At least no one could see what he was wearing underneath. He could go to school in his underwear if he wanted to.

Not that he wanted to, of course.

Stuart's family was eating breakfast when he came downstairs.

"Good morning," said his father cheerfully. He was going off to his job as a carpet cleaner.

"Good morning," said his mother cheerfully. She was going off to her job as a beautician.

"Good morning," said Aunt Bubbles cheerfully. She was going off to her job as a baker.

"I don't think it's a good morning," answered Stuart glumly. He was going off to be a total flop as a third grader.

I don't think it's a good morning!

VERY
BAD
DaY

Stuart had a lot to worry about, so he spread it out.

On the bus ride he worried about the bathroom thing, of course. And what if he were the shortest kid in the class?

Climbing up the big steps to school, he worried that his fives might come out backward while he was at the blackboard. And what if someone brought egg salad for lunch, and the smell made him throw up?

Dragging himself down the long hall to room 3B he worried about getting locked inside his

locker. And what if a wasp were hiding inside his juice carton at snack time and stung him, and his lip swelled up like a water balloon?

Stuart found the seat with his name tag and began worrying about the bathroom thing again. If worrying were a sport, he would have a neck full of gold medals by now.

"Good morning, children," said the teacher. "My name is Mrs. Spindles. Would anyone like to start by sharing something for Our Big Interesting World?"

A girl in the front row bounced up and down in her

seat so hard that a bunch of barrettes went flying. But she had about a hundred left in her hair.

"Yes, Olivia?" Mrs. Spindles called on her.

"My daddy went away on important business last week. He brought me back this pocketbook. It has real plastic diamonds on it."

"This used to be a muffin," said a boy named Nacho, proudly holding up a green lump. "I saved it under my bed all summer!"

Everyone in the class said, "*Cool, Nacho,*" except for Olivia, who was still looking for her barrettes.

Stuart smacked his head and groaned. Our Big Interesting World was the third grade name for show-and-tell. He wished he had something interesting to show. Like the false teeth he had found in the trash yesterday. Or the squashed toad from his driveway. Then all the kids would say, "*Cool, Stuart.*"

But wait! He did have something to show! Something so great that all the kids would fight over who could be his friend.

Stuart's hand shot up. He jumped around in his seat. If he'd been wearing barrettes they would have gone flying into the next classroom.

"Yes, Stuart?" Mrs. Spindles said. "Do you have something interesting to show us?"

"*Yesss!*" shouted Stuart as he ran to the front of the room. This was going to be great!

"I made this cape!" Stuart told the class. "I stapled a hundred ties together, and it's magic!

Every day I have a new adventure. And look! I put a secret purple pocket inside."

Stuart whipped open his cape very dramatically. He had practiced this in front of the mirror a lot.

He waited for the kids to say, "*Awesome!*" or "*Wow!*" or "*Cool, Stuart!*"

He waited for a long time. The room was so silent Stuart wondered if his ears had stopped working.

He felt an odd breeze. He looked down and froze in horror.

The awful new outfit had disappeared, just as he had wished. But now he was wearing nothing but his underpants. In front of the entire class!

He snapped his cape shut, but it was too late. All the kids began to laugh. When Stuart was embarrassed, his ears got embarrassed. As the kids laughed, he could feel his ears begin to blow up, like sausages on a grill.

Bigger and redder and hotter they grew, until suddenly the room went quiet again.

"Wow!" said Olivia. "Exactly the color of my Malibu Sunset Fashion barrettes."

"Wow!" said Nacho, holding two pieces of red construction paper up to his head. "Giant mutant alien radar ears."

"Wow!" said the rest of the kids.

Stuart fled back to his seat and buried his head in his arms. He kept it there for the rest of the morning.

At recess, he hid behind an extra-fat pine tree.

At lunch, he pretended to be extremely busy counting his raisins.

On the bus ride home, he put his lunchbox on the seat beside him and stared out the window so no one would sit with him.

He would never make a friend now. Not after this morning. But so what? He had a really good friend in his old town, and look what happened. He had to move away.

Besides, the kids here looked like a lot of trouble. If he made friends with Olivia he'd just spend his whole life looking for her barrettes, or admiring her pocketbooks. If he made friends with Nacho he'd have to watch out for moldy food.

No, it was better this way. He had a maniac cat that he loved. He had met the trash collector yesterday, and they were going to be partners in saving junk. And he had his cape. All he had to do was be a little more careful about what he wished for from now on.

DAY TWO

A brilliant idea woke Stuart up at the crack of dawn. "Today I'm going to bring in something so interesting for Our Big Interesting World that all the kids will forget what happened yesterday," he told One-Tooth.

Stuart crept downstairs. Right away, he found a potato that looked just like his first grade piano teacher. He found an enormous hairball that One-Tooth had spit up.

These were wonderful
things, of course, but most
kids had seen potatoes and
hairballs. To make up for
what had happened yester-
day, he would need something they had never
seen before.

He raced outside and grabbed a shovel. He
dug a nice, deep, round hole. It was an excellent
hole, one of his best. But all that was in it was
dirt. No gold, no jewels, no mysterious bones.
No treasureful stuff at all.

Stuart dug another hole. Nothing but dirt. Again.

And again, and again, and again.

Plenty of holes. Plenty of dirt.
Plenty of nothing to bring in for
Our Big Interesting World.

Stuart dropped his shovel. He was getting worried.

Great things had been happening to him since he had made his cape. He had grown toast, he had flown, some animals had come over to play.

But lately, not-so-great things had been happening. Yesterday, his clothes had disappeared.

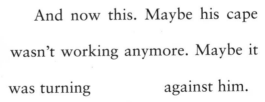

And now this. Maybe his cape wasn't working anymore. Maybe it was turning against him.

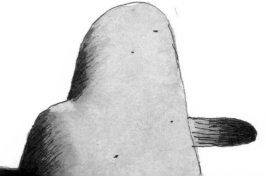

stuuuuaaaaart

"Stuuuuu-aaaart!
Time for breakfast!"

Aunt Bubbles's voice
was very small, and Stuart
could barely see his own
house in the distance. He must have been digging for a
long time.

He bent down to pick up his shovel. It was stuck.
He tugged and pulled it free, but something was caught
on the end.

It was a hole! A hole had peeled out of the ground
and was dangling from his shovel! This had never
happened before. But of course, he had
never had a cape before.

The hole was beautiful and deli-
cate, like a bubble with the top cut off.

Carefully, Stuart lifted it from the shovel and blew the dirt off. He folded it up and put it into the pocket of his cape.

Inside, Stuart drank three tall glasses of orange juice. Digging was thirsty work. "I have a hole in my pocket," he told his family.

"A big one?" asked his mother.

"Yep," Stuart answered proudly. "Nice and round, too."

"Don't put any money in it," warned his father.

"I wasn't going to," Stuart said.

"I don't have time to sew it up today," said Aunt Bubbles.

"I don't want you to sew it up," Stuart explained. He smeared a glump of jam over his toast and shook his head. Grown-ups.

All through Our Big Interesting World, Stuart suffered in silent gloom. One girl took off her shoe and

showed where a snake had almost
bitten her. A boy with braces showed
his collection of things that had
gotten stuck in them. *These kids probably have*

 *hundreds of friends*, Stuart
thought miserably.

If only he had more time, he
probably could have found some-
thing amazing. By now, all the kids would be crawling
all over themselves trying to be his friend. "Hey,
Stuart," they'd say. "Show us that amazing thing you
found again!" Stuff like that. Stuart laid his head on his
desk to imagine what it would be like.

Just then, one of the big kids knocked on the door
and handed Mrs. Spindles a note. Mrs. Spindles read
the note. She gasped and clutched at her throat. Her
eyes grew so large that Stuart wondered if they were
going to pop out of her head and go zinging across

the classroom. He would really like to see something like that.

"Attention, class!" Mrs. Spindles cried. "I have an emergency announcement!"

"*Holes!*" she read. "Hundreds and hundreds of holes! Neighborhoods have been finding them all morning. Detectives and scientists have been called in. Be on the alert today, and report anything unusual."

Mrs. Spindles dropped the note. "Oh, my dearest blue heavens!" she wailed. "Whatever could it be?"

"Hailstones, probably," Olivia said. "I'm going to have to wear a lot more barrettes."

"Giant earth-worms," Nacho said. "We're going to need some really big robins to eat them!"

All the kids had lots of ideas for what could have made so many holes. Each idea made Stuart feel worse.

Finally he raised his hand. "Maybe it

was a kid," he said in a voice that came out a little squeakier than he wanted. "Maybe a plain old regular kid was just digging around, looking for something."

"That is quite impossible, of course," Mrs. Spindles frowned. "Stuart, this is a very serious situation, and it is not the time for jokes."

Stuart's head hurt. This was turning into a rotten day. His arms were just about falling off from all the digging. He still hadn't found anything no one had ever seen before. The teacher thought he was making jokes.

And then he realized he had an even bigger problem: all that orange juice. He checked the clock — the bell wouldn't ring for hours. He'd never make it. He raised his hand. "I have to use the bathroom."

"It's at the end of the hall, next to the teachers' room," Mrs. Spindles told him.

Stuart wrote the directions down. They sounded simple, but he wasn't fooled. He knew simple things

could get tricky fast. *I will not get lost; I will not get lost,* he repeated to himself all the way.

And he didn't. There at the end of the hall, right next to the teachers' room was the boys' bathroom. But of course getting lost was only one of the things that could go wrong. Getting stuck inside was another.

Stuart used the bathroom faster than anyone had ever used it before in the history of the world. He

washed his hands even faster. He was almost out of there, but his heart began to squeeze in fear. *I will not get stuck inside; I will not get stuck inside*, he told his worried mirror face.

By the time Stuart dried his hands, he was a teeny bit panicked. He tore across the room, skidded to the door, and yanked the handle, *hard*.

Too hard.

Stuart stared at the door handle in his hand and tried not to cry. He didn't really care about being locked inside the boys' room. But pretty soon Mrs. Spindles would notice he was missing. She'd find out

STUCK

the door was stuck, and she'd call the firemen to get him out. It would probably be on the evening news. No one would ever want to be the friend of someone like him.

He was eight years old, and his life was ruined.

Stuart leaned his head against the wall and stroked his cape sadly. He had made the cape so interesting things would happen to him, but this was not what he had had in mind.

He wished he could just crawl into a hole and disappear.

And then it occurred to him: maybe he could.

Very gently, Stuart pulled the hole from his pocket. He shook it out and spread it against the wall. A little tunnel appeared. It was too dark to see anything beyond, but he took a deep breath and squeezed himself through. Anywhere was better than the boys' bathroom.

Stuart poked his head out the other side of the tunnel.

The room beyond was loud and full of teachers. A bunch of them were watching cartoons on television. A few were reading comic books on the floor with their feet on the walls. Two of them were jumping on a couch, making faces at each other. Giant boxes of doughnuts were scattered all around, and everybody was chomping gum or puffing cigars like crazy. Signs all over the room read: NO KIDS ALLOWED!

Wow, thought Stuart, *so this is the teachers' room!* One teacher stuffed three doughnuts into his mouth all at once, then stuck out his tongue. The others laughed and clapped him on the back. A teacher next to him made a rude noise. The others laughed and clapped her on the back, too.

Just then the door opened and Mrs. Spindles ran in. Someone hit her with a spitball. Mrs. Spindles hurled a doughnut back. "I can't play," she said. "One of my students got locked in the boys' room."

Mrs. Spindles picked up a phone and dialed. "Hello, hello!" she cried. "Code 3 at Punbury Elementary! Send the firemen right away!" Then she ran out of the room.

Stuart gulped in horror. He had to get back to the classroom, right now — but how? He couldn't just walk through the door, or jump out a window. There was only one thing that might work. . . .

Before he could worry about everything that might go wrong, he dropped to the floor. He reached behind him and peeled off the hole. Then he crawled to the nearest wall, slapped the hole against it, and made his escape into the hall.

Back in room 3B, Mrs. Spindles was nowhere to be seen. Stuart knew this was his big chance to turn all his bad luck into good. He climbed onto her desk. "I have something to show for Our Big Interesting World!" he announced. "Something you have never seen before!"

Stuart led the kids down the hall. One by one, he showed them the hole into the teachers' room. One by one they bent down and looked through it. He could hardly wait to see their reactions.

And then one by one, they stood up and stared at Stuart as though he were crazy.

Stuart bent down and looked into the teachers' room. It was dark and totally empty inside. Just the way he suddenly felt when he realized everyone had left him there alone.

Stuart walked back to 3B as slowly as a person could walk without actually standing still. At this rate, he hoped, the other kids might be in fourth grade by the time he got there. On the way, he passed an exit. He stopped to poke his head out the door, wishing he could just run away.

There in the parking lot were all the teachers. They were watching a crew of firemen putting away their ladders. The chief was talking to Mrs. Spindles.

"The darnedest thing. There was no one in the boys' room at all. But it's a good thing you called. We found two more of the Punbury Holes!"

Another fireman joined them. "Yep. One in the boys' room, one in the teachers' room. Right through

the walls! Whoever did this is probably a dangerous criminal!"

Stuart ran outside. He didn't want someone else to be blamed for what he did. "Wait," he cried. "I made the holes!"

Everyone turned to stare at Stuart. A man stepped forward. "I am the principal," he said. "You have obviously just had a very bad shock. In fact, we all have, so we are going to dismiss school early today."

"But really, it's because of my cape . . . " Stuart tried again.

"The principal is right, Stuart," said Mrs. Spindles. "You'll feel much better tomorrow. You might as well go home now."

Stuart decided to walk so he wouldn't have to face the other kids on the bus. With every step, his cape seemed to grow heavier and heavier, until he could hardly drag himself along. He sat down to rest outside Stanley the Trash Collector's barn, and his cape hung around him like a frown.

"Hi, Stuart," said Stanley. "You look as sad as yesterday's trash."

Stuart told him about his day. "I think my cape isn't working anymore. I think it's making me unlucky. Maybe I should just throw it away."

"People throw stuff away too quickly," Stanley
said. "You've got to give it a chance."

"I guess I could try wearing it one more day," Stuart
sighed. "After all, things couldn't possibly get any
worse."

DAY THREE

There should be a rule, Stuart thought, *that if you are late to school no one should talk about it. Being late is embarrassing enough.*

"You are late this morning, Stuart," Mrs. Spindles said, as if anyone in the room hadn't noticed this.

"I'm sorry," Stuart said, feeling his ears begin to blow up. "I had to fill in about a hundred holes. I'm the one who dug them, not some dangerous criminal!"

"Oh, Stuart!" laughed Mrs. Spindles. "Stop pulling my leg!"

Stuart sank into his seat, stunned. *Why would she say that?* He wasn't even close enough to pull her leg. Plus, why would he want to?

He sighed. It was hopeless. Even though he was wearing all his clothes, and even though he had remembered not to drink anything this morning, he was *still* going to have a bad day.

Math was first. Today's lesson was the number twelve. Most of the kids already knew about twelve. They knew it was also called a dozen. They knew it was ten plus two. Or six plus six.

Stuart knew about twelve, too. So far so good. And then Mrs. Spindles said something so wonderful Stuart could hardly believe his ears.

"Now class," was the wonderful thing she said, "I want you each to draw a picture for twelve."

Finally! Here was his chance to make up for all the bad starts! He had been the best drawer in his old school. If another kid drew a mouse, people might think it was a zucchini squash or a hat. There was no way to tell. But if Stuart drew a mouse, everyone knew it was a mouse. Even grown-ups. That's how good he was.

He wanted to draw something really fabulous now. Something so good all the kids would fight with one another to see who could be the best friend of such a great artist. He took his special drawing pencil from the pocket of his cape and began.

Stuart worked so hard he lost track of time. This happens to artists a lot. Pretty soon all the other kids were crowded around his desk to see what was taking so long. Here is what they saw:

stuart

Twelve students! There were twelve students in Mrs. Spindles' third-grade class. And every one of them was on Stuart's paper!

Stuart knew it was one of his best drawings. Very detailed. Still, his heart thudded with dread. Drawing people could be tricky. You never knew how people might react. They might get mad if you left off their ears or made their feet look a tiny bit like bananas.

"There's me!" shouted Olivia. "Stuart drew all my barrettes!"

"Awesome!" cried Nacho. "My feet look like bananas!"

All the kids were so happy to find themselves in Stuart's drawing.

"Let's show Mrs. Spindles," they said.

Stuart was secretly very proud. But he just said, "Well, okay. If you want to."

But where *was* Mrs. Spindles?

Olivia called down the hall. Nacho checked the playground.

"Just like your drawing," Nacho said. "Twelve kids and no teacher."

Stuart looked at his drawing. He looked at his pencil. He looked at his cape. *Of course.*

"Don't worry," he told the other kids calmly. As if losing a teacher were the most normal thing in the world. "Things like this happen to me all the time. I'll just have to *draw* Mrs. Spindles to bring her back. No problem."

But there was a problem: No room on the paper.

The twelve students filled up the classroom. The swing set filled up the playground.

There was only one place left to put her.

"Help!" Mrs. Spindles' voice floated down into the classroom. "I don't know what's gotten into me. I seem to have climbed up onto the roof!"

"Don't worry," Stuart called up to her. "I'll draw you a ladder."

But he couldn't do it! He couldn't draw a ladder,

even though he had been the best drawer in his old school. *Too many straight lines.*

Stuart tried again. And again. And again. He tried

twelve times. Twelve ladders, each too crooked to use.

Stuart began to panic. Probably no kid in the history of third grade had ever put a teacher on the roof. He was going to jail for life, unless he could think up a *terrific* idea.

And then he did just that.

"Hold on!" he called up to Mrs. Spindles. "You'll be on the ground in a few seconds." Stuart erased Mrs. Spindles' old legs and gave her some new, reach-the-ground ones.

Mrs. Spindles's new long legs waved wildly past the windows. The other kids dove for cover under their desks.

"Oh, dear!" cried Mrs. Spindles. "What in the world has happened? How will I tie my shoes?"

How will she walk around? wondered Stuart. *How will she fit in the classroom? And whatever made me think this was a good idea?*

"Hang on," he called, trying to sound cheerful. He got a big piece of paper. "I'm going to start all over."

Stuart bit his bottom lip to concentrate. Very carefully he drew Mrs. Spindles inside the classroom. With normal legs.

He drew twelve desks, and a flag, and a chalkboard. He drew Smiling Ed, the class turtle, and Sparky and

Pal, the hamsters. It was the best drawing of his career. But it wasn't done.

Stuart grinned. Outside, where there was plenty of room, he drew twelve kids . . .

ALL PLAYING <u>TOGETHER</u>!!!

Stepping onto the bus going home, Stuart had the feeling something was missing. It wasn't a bad something-was-missing feeling, like if you forgot to put your pants on. It was a good something-was-missing feeling, like if the poison ivy between your toes were finally gone.

He took a seat in front of Nacho and tried to think what it was.

Nacho tugged on his cape. "Will you draw *me* some longer legs?" he asked Stuart. "Like you did with Mrs. Spindles?"

Stuart studied Nacho. Nacho was short, like he was, but at least Stuart had a tall neck. Nacho was just plain short, all over. In fact, he was the only kid in third grade shorter than Stuart. This was too bad for Nacho, but very good for Stuart.

That's what was missing! Stuart wasn't *worried* anymore. He wasn't the shortest kid in the class. He

hadn't thrown up from an egg salad smell, he hadn't

forgotten everything he'd learned in second grade, and

he hadn't gotten stuck in the bathroom. At least not for

very long. And even though he hadn't made any friends,

the other kids had played with him.

It felt weird not having anything to worry about, but good. *Still*, Stuart would have drawn Nacho longer legs if he could have. Even though it would have made *him* the shortest kid in third grade.

"You can put sandwiches in your shoes to make yourself taller," he told Nacho. "That's what I do sometimes. Ham and cheese is the best; tuna fish is not so good. But I can't draw you longer legs. My cape doesn't work that way. I only get one thing a day. One adventure."

"That's okay," Nacho said. "I can wait until tomorrow."

Stuart shook his head. "It doesn't work like that, either. It's a *different* thing every day."

Just then, Olivia stuck her legs across the aisle. "My legs are exactly the right length," she said. "But if I had longer hair I could wear more barrettes. So tomorrow you can draw me with longer hair,

right down to my ankles. That would be a *different* thing."

Stuart sighed. It was hard to have to keep saying no. "I'm sorry. Every day the different thing that happens is a surprise to me. I never know what it will be, and I don't get to choose." He turned his head to the window. Nacho and Olivia wouldn't want to talk to him anymore.

Nacho tugged on his cape again. "I get it. It's like the ties in your cape. Each one is different."

Stuart hadn't thought of this. Nacho was right. Olivia leaned over and whacked him with her pocketbook.

"I *like* surprises," she said. "Surprises are *presents*."

Olivia was right, too.

Olivia and Nacho stood up to leave at the bus stop before Stuart's.

"Tomorrow is Saturday," Nacho said. "We'll come over early."

"Right," Olivia agreed. "So we don't miss anything."

When Stuart jumped off the bus, his cape streamed around him in a gigantic grin.

How to do a ~~terific~~ really good portrait of me (stuart)

by Stuart

(1) Begin with my head and shoulders

(2) add my glasses and ears (not too big)

(3) then put the nose (thin) and eyes (smart)

(4) next my hair (That's the tricky part)

HAPPY

NOT HAPPY AT ALL!

hello!

(5) Finally, add the mouth, cheeks, arms and eyebrows (very important) With these, you can make a lot of different expressions for your favorite HERO! Keep my portrait in your room (especially if you are a GIRL!)

note: Don't forget to draw at least a dozen fingers!

CHICAGO PUBLIC LIBRARY
SULZER REGIONAL
4455 N. LINCOLN
CHICAGO, IL 60625